Humphrey's

Playtime

Sally Hunter

Humphrey likes playing with

his special painted animals...

...painting a lovely picture
for Mummy to put on
the kitchen wall...

...finding little creatures

and taking them for a
trip to the shops......

...being very, very brave

and saving everybody...

"...galloping on Henry Horse..."

...getting lost at sea
with lots of monsters...

...making roads in the mud for the trucks... and tractors

...and cars...

...and riding his Big Boy Bike.

But best of all, Humphrey likes...

looking after...

...cuddling...

...sharing with...

...and loving...Mopx

To Lucy
Love
Sal x

PUFFIN BOOKS

Published by the Penguin Group:
London, New York, Australia, Canada, India, New Zealand and South Africa
Penguin Books Ltd, Registered Offices: Harmondsworth, Middlesex, England

On the World Wide Web at: www.penguin.com

First published 2001

1 3 5 7 9 10 8 6 4 2

Copyright © Sally Hunter, 2001

Printed in China by Imago

ISBN 0-140-56746-1

To find out more about Humphrey's world, visit the web site at:
www.humphreys-corner.com